Books by Paige Sleuth

CRASH
in CHERRY
HILLS

COZY CAT

A CAPER

MYSTERY BOOK

23

PAIGE SLEUTH

CHAPTER ONE

66 This here is the best SUV on the market today," the Rockport Rides salesman named DJ said. "She's got everything you need for the smoothest driving experience on the road. Rain sensors, seat warmers, dual temperature controls. You name it, she's got it."

Katherine Harper studied DJ from a few feet away. With a strong, healthy build and jet black hair that couldn't possibly contain less than half a tube of hair gel, he couldn't be that old, maybe twenty-two or twenty-three at the most. But his confident, almost cocky, air and predatory smile gave Kat the impression he had been selling cars for years. He was the type of person she could picture slipping one-sided clauses into his contracts on a regular basis. If she were the one in the market for a new vehicle instead of her friend, she would have already driven to the next dealership by now.

"So." DJ rubbed his palms together as he graced Imogene Little with that shark-like smile. "Whaddaya say? You wanna take her for a spin?"

Imogene frowned. "I don't know. Seat warmers? It seems a little unnecessary."

DJ pointed at the sun shining down on them. "You only say that because it's the middle of June. Come December when you're driving through the Central Washington snow with toasty warm buns, you'll be happy you didn't scrimp."

Imogene fingered a piece of auburn hair that had slipped loose from her ponytail. "I'm just not sure I need all that."

"Well, seat warmers aren't the only thing this baby has going for her. She can also make calls and send text messages with nothing more than a few simple voice commands."

Imogene wrinkled her nose. "I don't use my phone while driving."

"That's my point. You don't need to use your phone. This vehicle *becomes* your phone as soon as you start the engine and she syncs up."

"I really prefer to pull over if I need to make a call."

"You'll love this next feature then. This peach has got a dedicated charger port built right into the console. No need to rely on ancient technology like cigarette lighters and clunky special cords. Nope, you just plug in your standard charger cable, and by the time you're ready to make that call you'll have a full battery at your disposal."

"Or I could continue to plug my phone in at home every night like I do now," Imogene replied. "Easy-peasy."

DJ arched his eyebrows. "And what happens when you forget one day? You want to end up lost somewhere with no battery life?"

"Given how I rarely venture outside Cherry Hills town limits, I'm sure I'd manage." Imogene turned toward Kat. "What do you think, Kat?"

"I think it's a little much," Kat said, figuring that was what Imogene wanted to hear. When her friend had asked her to tag along for 'moral support,' Kat hadn't known what she meant. But after seeing DJ in action, she was starting to understand why Imogene hadn't wanted to shop for cars alone.

DJ must have decided there was no point in continuing to push this particular vehicle. He started down the aisle of available cars. "All right. I hear you. And I've got a gem down here that's bound to be more your style. You're gonna love this one."

Kat and Imogene followed him, Imogene with a bounce in her step and Kat more grudgingly.

DJ stopped in front of a mint green SUV. "Here she is! Does this beauty scream value or what? She's still got all the basics, but if it's simple you want, this is your gal."

Imogene's lips puckered. "It's bright green."

"Enchanted forest. It's one of the hottest colors on the market now. Puts a person in mind of nature and meadows and acres of farmland. And didn't you say you'll be using your new ride to transport livestock?"

"Rescue animals," Imogene corrected. "Cats and dogs, not cows."

DJ smacked the SUV's hood with one palm. "Well, then, this baby's perfect! She's designed to comfortably seat eight."

"Hmm." Imogene peered through the rear window. "How big is the cargo area?"

"As spacious as they come."

"Can I see it?"

Kat didn't miss how DJ's smile faltered. No doubt the cargo area wasn't quite as roomy as the salesman wanted them to believe.

He was saved from having to respond when a black cat crawled out from underneath the car. With an exaggerated yawn, the feline sat on the pavement and looked at them. From here Kat could see a tiny white patch on each of his front legs, and when he placed his paws side by side the spots merged into one.

"Well, hello there," Imogene said, her face lighting up. "And who are you?"

"That's Moxie," DJ said. "He lives here."

"You have a resident cat? How delightful!" Imogene crouched down to offer Moxie her hand.

"He was a feral who used to show up every other day. Then my mom started feeding him about a year ago, and now he never leaves."

"How come Sally Jo doesn't bring him home?"

"Dad's allergic."

Imogene patted Moxie's head before standing back up and facing Kat. "DJ's father owns this place. Damian Rockport and I went to school together in the sixties and seventies, back when Rockport Rides belonged to Damian's own father."

"Ah." Kat had been wondering why Imogene hadn't hightailed it to another dealership already. Apparently she shared a history with the owner.

"Where are Damian and Sally Jo this afternoon?" Imogene asked DJ. "I'd like to say hi if they're around."

"Mama's up to her eyeballs in paperwork," DJ replied. "Not sure about Dad. I saw him drive off not too long ago, but I don't know what he's up to or when he'll be back. He tends to do his own thing around here."

Imogene grinned. "He always has."

DJ chuckled, and Kat was surprised to note how much more personable he seemed when he wasn't involved in a hard sell.

"So," DJ said, straightening up. He patted the SUV. "What do you think about this beauty?"

And the shark was back, Kat thought.

Imogene perused the window sticker. "It's a bit pricey."

Moxie rubbed against Imogene's ankles a few times before sauntering down the aisle.

When the cat reached a dark blue model several yards away, he jumped on the hood, sat down, and stared right at Imogene as if to say, 'Here's your new car. You're welcome.'

"Oh, look at this one." Imogene scooted closer to Moxie's selection. "It's quite nice, isn't it?" She glanced at the sticker. "And affordable."

DJ joined her by the SUV. "That's an older model, but she's the best of her year. Fully keyless, and the smoothest riding experience you'll find anywhere. Start 'er up, and she purrs just like a cat."

Moxie began purring as if to demonstrate what they could expect to hear from the engine.

Imogene glanced over her shoulder. "What do you think, Kat?"

Kat surveyed the vehicle. "It looks nice. And roomy."

"I promise you can't go wrong with this one," DJ said. "She's a trade-in, three years old, but everything's like brand-new. Not much mileage on her either. Hey, here comes our star mechanic now. You can get the inside scoop on how well she runs direct from our expert."

DJ waved over the tall, lanky man who had emerged from the side of the dealership. An unlit cigarette dangled from the man's mouth, and he held a lighter in one hand. Moxie's nose twitched as if he could already smell the tobacco burning.

"Teddy!" DJ called out. "Come and give these ladies the skinny on this baby's engine." He slapped the SUV's hood, causing Moxie to jump.

Teddy stared at DJ. Kat thought he might pretend not to have heard the car salesman, but then he slipped his lighter into the pocket of his dirty blue coveralls and ambled in their direction.

"What do you need, DJ?" Teddy said, tucking his cigarette behind one ear.

DJ clapped Teddy on the shoulder. "These ladies are interested in this beauty here, but they'd like an expert's assurance they aren't getting swindled."

"Oh." Teddy looked startled that someone cared about his opinion. "The engine's all right, if that's what you're asking. Nothing really specia—"

"Teddy here performs periodic checks on every car in this lot himself," DJ interjected. "He wouldn't let us sell a lemon. That would ruin my dad's reputation."

Imogene reached out and stroked Moxie's

back. "Perhaps I could take it for a test drive."

DJ nodded with such gusto Kat was sure he'd develop a crick in his neck. "That's imminently doable," he said.

The sound of a car honking interrupted the conversation. DJ, Teddy, Imogene, and Kat all turned toward the road, where a red sedan was speeding down the street in front of the dealership.

DJ frowned. "That's Dad's car."

Moxie meowed as if he too recognized the vehicle.

"He'd better slow down," Teddy said. "That curve coming up is a doozy."

Imogene opened her mouth as though to say something, but her jaw just kept dropping. She had the same horrified expression on her face that Kat imagined was on her own. It was becoming increasingly clear that the car wasn't going to slow down.

Moxie let out an anguished meow before darting off. Kat didn't see where he went, barely registering the streak of black out of the corner of her eye. Her gaze was fixed on the red sedan.

The car careened off the pavement, narrowly missing one tree only to slam into another. The sickening sound of crunching metal sent Kat's stomach dropping to the ground.

No one moved. The four of them continued to stare at the car as if waiting for the driver to open the door. When it became clear that wasn't going to happen, they all rushed forward at once.

CHAPTER TWO

The medics didn't take long to arrive, the police right behind them. After the EMTs pronounced Damian Rockport to be dead, Chief Kenny, the Cherry Hills Police Department chief, and Andrew Milhone, Kat's boyfriend and one of Cherry Hills' finest, instructed everyone to wait inside the dealership while they processed the scene.

Moxie must have figured police orders applied to him as well. The black cat had reappeared at some point and was now accompanying Kat, Imogene, DJ, and Teddy into the building. He didn't act like a feral, and Kat had to wonder if he'd had a home before he'd started spending all his time at Rockport Rides.

Once inside, Kat had a better understanding of why the feline liked this place so much. The showroom was one large area with floor-to-ceiling glass windows that spanned two sides of the building and gave the room a pleasant, open-air feel. The room's main attractions were two shiny new cars each positioned on a low dais. A couple desks sporting nothing more than some basic office supplies had been set up near one of the windows. Kat figured that was where the salespeople sealed their deals in ink. For the people behind the scenes, doors to the service area and several offices were built into the back wall. And the other side of the room featured a beverage station and a spacious seating area.

Kat opted to stand by the front window, where she had a good view of the police activity outside and, farther beyond, the scene of the crash. She could still see the gut-wrenching moment of impact in her head and hear the nauseating crunch of metal in her ears. She had never witnessed a car accident before and hoped she never would again.

Except, had it really been an accident? Several things bothered her. First, why had Damian been driving so fast? Surely he took that curve every day and knew when he needed to slow down. Second, the way he'd leaned on the horn as he'd barreled down the street wasn't natural. It suggested something might have been wrong with the car, something that had prevented Damian from avoiding that crash.

The whole incident was definitely troublesome.

A moan pulled Kat's attention to her left. A forty-something blond woman in a bright yellow sundress and matching high-heeled shoes sat in front of one of the sales desks. She had her arms folded across her stomach as she rocked back and forth in her chair, a pained look on her tear-streaked face.

"I can't believe the Lord has called my Damian home so soon," she cried out.

DJ occupied the seat next to her. He touched her arm. "I'm so sorry, Mama."

This must be Sally Jo, Kat thought, recalling how Imogene had asked about her not twenty minutes ago. Then, her biggest challenge had been a mounting pile of paperwork. Now she was facing life without her husband.

"I wish I knew what to do for you, Mama," DJ said. "But I'm at a loss."

Moxie didn't seem to have that problem.

The black cat zoomed toward Sally Jo and jumped into her lap as if he knew exactly what was needed in this situation. The tiny white patches on his front legs bobbed up and down as he began kneading her thigh.

Sally Jo stroked the cat with one hand, her long, fake, pink fingernails leaving parallel tracks in the animal's black fur. "Oh, Moxie." She sucked in and released several deep breaths. "You make me happier than a possum with a sweet potato, you know that? Here I was fixin' to break down faster than a Tin Lizzie with no gas in the gozzle and then you show up."

Kat didn't understand all that, but Moxie apparently did. He gazed up at Sally Jo with eyes half closed as he drank in her praise.

DJ evidently understood too. His nostrils widened a fraction before he withdrew his hand from his mother's arm and angled away from her. It was clear from his body language he didn't appreciate being made redundant by a cat.

Sally Jo reached over and patted DJ's knee. "DJ, be a good boy and fetch me Moxie's treats, will you?"

DJ grumbled something as he stood up and trudged across the showroom floor. Sally Jo watched him until he disappeared through a door in the back. When she turned back around, her eyes locked with Kat's.

"Oh, hello," she said. "Have you been standin' there long?"

"Hi. Sorry." Kat held up her hands. "I didn't mean to intrude."

Sally Jo dabbed underneath her wet eyes with a tissue. Moxie tried to help by touching her cheek with his paw, his concern eliciting a faint smile from Sally Jo.

Kat stood there, feeling helpless. "Is there anything I can do for you?"

"I don't see what anybody can do." Sally Jo shut her eyes and drew in a ragged breath.

Moxie released a soft cooing sound and snuggled closer to the widow. She hugged him as her shoulders shook with grief.

Kat was just looking around for a reason to excuse herself when Sally Jo spoke again.

"You were here when it happened," she said. It wasn't a question but a statement.

Kat's eyes automatically slid toward the window. "I was."

"I saw you outside with Imogene Little. I'm Sally Jo Rockport-Dubois, Damian's wife. Damian's widow." Her face crumpled. "I'm such a mess. This accident has left me as shaken as a strawberry daiquiri."

"That was no accident," a male voice announced.

Kat and Sally Jo whipped around. Teddy stood a few feet away, his hands clasped in front of him. Kat had lost track of him and Imogene after they'd entered the building and had no idea how long he'd been standing there.

"That was no accident," Teddy said again. "Somebody killed Mr. Rockport."

Sally Jo gasped, one bejeweled hand floating to her chest. Moxie let out an equally alarmed cry, although whether the cat was responding to Teddy's statement or Sally Jo's distress was debatable.

Teddy stepped closer. "Sorry to be the one to tell you this, ma'am, but somebody cut the brake lines in Mr. Rockport's car."

Sally Jo looked too stunned to say anything. Moxie pressed the top of his head against her chin as if to keep her jaw from hitting the floor.

"I just checked the spot where Mr. Rockport parks," Teddy continued. "There's brake fluid on the pavement."

Kat's heart rate quickened as she replayed the crash in her mind's eye. Faulty brakes certainly fit with the scenario she'd witnessed.

Sally Jo's gaze drifted out the window before she jerked her eyes back to Teddy. "Damian must've spilled coffee out there this mornin'. That man could trip over his own shadow if he wasn't careful. That must've been what you saw."

Teddy shook his head. "That was no coffee."

"Are you sure the brake lines were cut?" Kat asked. "Could they have broken by themselves?"

"No, ma'am. I inspected that car myself just this morning, same as I do every Saturday. I would've noticed any hardware defects before now. The lines had to have been cut. It's the only explanation. And another thing, they couldn't have been cut clear through. This had to have been a slow leak. Otherwise Mr. Rockport would have noticed something was wrong before he drove off the lot."

Kat's skin prickled as she rotated back toward the window and refocused on the police activity outside. She wondered if Chief Kenny and Andrew had figured out yet that they might have a murder on their hands.

CHAPTER THREE

"Sally Jo!"

The high-pitched cry was followed by the click of stiletto heels against tile as a woman rushed into the dealership. In those ridiculous shoes she had to be over six feet tall. She was probably closer to seven if you included her teased-up blond hair.

Moxie scrambled out of Sally Jo's lap and hotfooted it to the other side of the sales floor. Kat wasn't sure if it was the woman's screeching tone, her teetering heels, or the cloud of perfume that followed her into the room that the cat found most alarming.

Sally Jo jumped out of her chair. "Beulah!"

With arms outstretched, the women rushed

toward each other. Cries and shrieks ensued. Kat winced, the cacophony threatening to burst an eardrum. The women's voices had the same pitch as an air raid siren.

Kat felt a tap on her arm. Imogene had returned from wherever she'd gone and now stood beside her, her eyebrows raised. She tilted her head toward the women, a questioning look on her face. Kat shrugged.

Beulah pulled away from Sally Jo. "Sally Jo, what on earth is this I hear about Damian meetin' his maker?"

Sally Jo's eyes filled with fresh tears. "It's true."

"My word. When Damian Junior phoned me I thought he was just yankin' my chain. Took me longer than a preacher's minute 'fore I realized he wasn't tryin' to pull one over on his Auntie Beulah."

"Oh, Beulah." Sally Jo choked on a sob. "I'm at my wits' end. I can't believe the Lord has called my Damian to him already. I nearly wet my britches when I happened to look out that window there yonder as Damian came whippin' 'round that bend in the road like Hell's fire was after him."

Beulah's blue eyes widened. "Well, butter

my behind and call me a biscuit! You saw it happen?"

Sally Jo nodded as she dabbed at her eyes.

"Oh my word!" Beulah looked between Teddy, Imogene, and Kat. "Did all y'all see it too?"

"We sure did," Teddy said.

Beulah wrapped her arms around Sally Jo again. "Oh, honey, no wonder you're fallin' to pieces faster than a granola sandwich."

DJ emerged from the office. He hovered a few feet behind his mother, looking reluctant to interrupt the embrace.

Beulah caught sight of him over Sally Jo's shoulder. "Damian Junior!" She released Sally Jo and flung her arms in his direction. "Look at you, you poor thing! You come give your Auntie Beulah a hug."

DJ shifted his feet. "I'm okay, Aunt Beulah."

"Hogwash. You just lost your daddy! That brave face of yours don't fool your auntie even a lick. Now come and get some of this sugar before I give myself a cavity."

DJ flinched as Beulah lunged toward him. Something shot out of his hands, and tiny particles exploded all over the showroom. One hit Kat square in the forehead before clattering to the floor. She looked down at her feet, her eyes landing on a cat treat.

Moxie hurried over from wherever he'd been hiding. The black cat zigzagged around the room, his paws skidding on the slick floor as he raced to gobble up the treats.

If he feared the humans would sweep up his smorgasbord before he had a chance to eat his fill he didn't need to worry. Sally Jo was oblivious, her face buried behind a tissue, and Beulah currently had DJ immobilized in a crushing embrace. Kat thought she might even be suffocating him from the way he was squirming.

When Beulah finally released him, DJ glanced around, an embarrassed flush working its way up his cheeks.

Teddy took a step forward. "You're Sally Jo's sister?"

"In the flesh, sugar." Beulah graced Teddy with a radiant smile. "You work for Damian?"

"I'm the full-time mechanic."

If Beulah was offended by how Teddy's gaze stayed glued to her bosoms, she didn't show it. Kat had to figure Beulah was used to men staring at her chest. Not only were her assets on the large side, but those shoes put her chest about level with the average man's eyes.

Sally Jo laid one hand on Beulah's forearm. "Teddy here says Damian's car wreck was no accident."

Beulah gasped. She stared at Teddy as if he'd sprouted horns above his ears.

"It's true," Teddy said. "There's brake fluid out where Mr. Rockport kept his car parked. Someone must have messed with his vehicle."

"Why, honey, you sound crazier than a hog sellin' pork at the Piggly Wiggly!" Beulah tottered toward Teddy and pressed her palm against his forehead. "You sure you ain't runnin' a fever?"

"No, ma'am."

Beulah pulled her hand back and planted it on her hip. "But who on God's green earth would want to harm Damian?"

Teddy shrugged. "Guess the police will have to figure out that part."

"Or Kat," Imogene piped up.

Kat nearly fell over at the mention of her name. She caught Imogene's eye and gave her head a subtle shake, but Imogene didn't appear to notice.

Beulah peered at Imogene down the bridge of her nose. "Excuse my manners. Do we know each other?"

Imogene shook her head. "Kat and I were here looking at cars when the crash happened."

"Imogene knows Damian from way back when they were both knee-high to a bullfrog," Sally Jo added.

"And Kat here is my friend," Imogene put in. "She's also an incorrigible snoop and a whiz at solving crimes."

"Is that so." Beulah looked Kat up and down, a dubious quirk to her lips.

"You won't find a sharper sleuth than Kat anywhere in Cherry Hills," Imogene said, beaming as brightly as a proud mother hen. "Why, I bet she has this whole thing solved before I drive her back to Cherry Hills Commons."

Kat's cheeks burned. She bowed her head and stared at the shiny showroom floor, wishing it would open up and swallow her whole.

With her gaze on the floor, Kat saw that Moxie was still busy packing away treats. She watched as he inched closer to Beulah before darting forward and clamping his teeth around a morsel positioned near the toe of her shoe. He carried his prize a safe distance away before chomping into it.

Beulah gave no indication that she noticed Moxie. Her eyes were fixed on something near the back of the room.

"Oh my word," Beulah said, pressing one hand against her chest. "Tell me I had one too many mimosas for lunch and that's not who I think it is."

Kat glanced across the sales floor. A twenty-something brunette in a black T-shirt and jeans had emerged from one of the back rooms. She seemed oblivious to everyone's stares as she made her way to the beverage station.

"That is her, ain't it?" Although Beulah had lowered her voice, it was still about twenty decibels higher than a whisper.

Sally Jo gave her a stiff nod.

Beulah stamped her foot. The clack of her heel against the tile sounded like a gunshot and sent the treat-scavenging Moxie fleeing for safety.

"Why, I don't believe it," Beulah said. "What's she still doin' piddlin' 'round here?"

Sally Jo squeezed her arm. "Don't make a fuss about it."

"You talking about Amy?" Teddy asked Beulah's chest.

"We sure are, sugar," Beulah replied.

"What did Amy do?" Imogene asked.

Beulah pursed her lips, her gaze zeroing in

on the brunette. "That woman over there dated my nephew, then for no good rhyme or reason dropped him quicker'n a pair of barbecue tongs left too long on the grill."

DJ turned beet red. "Aunt Beulah, do you have to tell that to everybody?"

"Why shouldn't I?"

"Because. It's embarrassing."

Beulah pinched DJ's cheek. "Oh, now, Damian Junior. You've got nothin' to be red-faced about. If anybody should be ashamed to show their face 'round here it's that she-devil who wouldn't recognize a good man if God himself stuck a bow on his head and delivered him on Christmas mornin'. And shame on Damian for not kickin' her to the curb when he had the chance!"

DJ shoved his hands in his pants pockets, his gaze falling to his shoes. Sally Jo sniffled as though she might be on the verge of tears again.

Beulah flushed. "Gracious, my mouth has run off to Alaska without me. I didn't mean to speak ill of the dead." She crossed herself. "Poor Damian, may he rest in peace."

Kat studied Amy across the room. Was it possible Damian had been thinking of letting her go because of how she'd treated his son? In that case, maybe she'd killed him as a preemptive measure.

Except, would killing Damian really provide Amy with any job security? It seemed just as likely that Sally Jo or DJ would fire her once they took over the business—assuming they were taking over the business.

Kat's breath hitched. Who *did* stand to inherit Rockport Rides now that Damian was gone? Because in her estimation, whoever took over was about to become very wealthy. The value of the car lot's inventory alone would be enough for a person to live on for most, if not all, of their lifetime.

Kat looked at Sally Jo, Damian's most likely heir. She had a hard time envisioning the dolled-up Southern belle fiddling underneath the hood of a car. Would Sally Jo even know what a brake line looked like? It seemed doubtful.

Or was Kat not giving the widow enough credit? Just because she wore pretty dresses and kept her nails manicured didn't mean she didn't know anything about automobiles. In fact, given her husband's line of work it was extremely likely she had picked up a thing or two about a car's inner workings over the years.

Maybe she had even learned enough to put her knowledge to diabolical use, if she so desired.

CHAPTER FOUR

Kat tried to keep up with Sally Jo and Beulah's chatter after they moved away from the topic of Amy, but the two had started jabbering a mile a minute and most of their Southern expressions didn't make any sense to Kat.

Apparently Kat wasn't the only one who found the sisters' conversation impossible to follow. Imogene drifted off to one side of the showroom to make a phone call, and Teddy disappeared into the service area. DJ was the only one who stayed put, interjecting a word or two here and there mostly because that was what seemed to be expected of him.

Nobody appeared to notice or care about the

brunette quietly crying on the other side of the room.

Kat walked over to where Amy sat on one of the plastic chairs set up in the beverage area. The young woman had her legs pulled up to her chest, her forehead resting on her knees.

"Are you okay?" Kat asked.

Amy lifted up her head. Her brown eyes were red-rimmed, and tear streaks marred her cheeks.

"Is there anything I can do for you?" Kat asked.

"No."

If the word had been spoken with malice or annoyance Kat would have let Amy grieve in peace. But despite the curtness of her reply, the young woman didn't sound averse to company. And Kat was reluctant to venture back to the other side of the showroom. Her ears needed a break.

Kat eased into a chair two seats away. "I'm sorry about Damian Rockport."

"Me too."

Amy grabbed the paper cup on the table beside her and tipped it above her lips. The way she knocked back her drink made Kat suspect there might be something other than soda in there. But unless someone had a liquor bottle hidden in one of the cabinets, the beverage station offered nothing stronger than coffee.

Moxie came strolling over, his pink tongue swiping at his lips. He laid down on the tile floor—his stomach undoubtedly bloated from too many treats—and worked on cleaning his whiskers.

Amy set the cup back down and faced Kat. "What did they say about me?"

"I'm sorry?" Kat said.

Amy jutted her chin across the room. "I heard Mrs. Rockport-Dubois and her sister talking about me when I came out here."

Kat wasn't surprised, given the women's shrill tones.

"What did they say?" Amy asked.

"Just that you dated DJ for a while."

"That's it?"

"That was the gist of it."

Kat held her breath, hoping Amy wouldn't press for details. But Amy seemed satisfied with that answer. For the first time, she smiled.

"I bet Mrs. Rockport-Dubois still can't believe anyone would break up with her precious son," Amy said.

"Her sister was the one who seemed more

incredulous."

"Oh, yeah. Ms. Dubois is a real drama queen. And her and Mrs. Rockport-Dubois are like this." Amy crossed her index and middle fingers.

Kat reclined in her chair, trying to get comfortable against the hard plastic. "They both seem pretty torn up about Damian's death."

Amy's face fell. "Yeah."

Moxie must have taken Kat's relaxed posture as an invitation to join her. The black cat rolled into a standing position and jumped into her lap.

"Mr. Rockport was a great guy," Amy said. "And he was pretty popular around town too. My main job here is to phone customers when their car is due for servicing or we think they might be interested in trading up. Most everybody I call seems to know Mr. Rockport on a personal level. They always ask about him." Amy scrutinized Kat. "Did you know Mr. Rockport?"

Kat shook her head. "I never met him."

"You're not from Cherry Hills?"

"I grew up here, but I moved away for about fifteen years. I've only been back since last summer."

"Well, nobody I know has a bad word to say about Mr. Rockport. I mean, he can be rather old-fashioned, but he's real nice." Amy bit her lip. "Or I guess I should say he *was* real nice."

"What do you mean by old-fashioned?" Kat asked.

"He thought women had their place, and men had theirs. That's why Mrs. Rockport-Dubois and I work the phones and files, and DJ and Teddy work the cars."

"So Sally Jo isn't an equal business partner?"

"No way. She isn't even a business partner at all. It's too bad too because she actually has a lot of ideas on how to drum up new business. But Mr. Rockport would never let her implement them. In his mind she's just a pretty face, someone he can use to lure in rich men with an eye for beautiful women and an even bigger eye for beautiful cars."

Kat petted Moxie as she scrutinized Sally Jo across the room. She had assumed the bright sundress and fake fingernails reflected the woman's personal style, but maybe Sally Jo wasn't as high-maintenance as she appeared. Maybe that was the persona Damian had created for her.

It made her wonder if Sally Jo had finally tired of being paraded around like eye candy and killed her husband so she could end his oppressive regime and start running Rockport Rides the way she wanted to once and for all. Murder was a messier option than divorce, but then again, perhaps divorce wouldn't have left her with a stake in the business.

Of course, Sally Jo wasn't the only suspect to consider.

"Amy," Kat said, "how did DJ get along with his father?"

Amy shrugged. "All right. Why?"

"Just curious." Kat paused, working out how to phrase her next question. "What happened between you and DJ anyway?"

"Nothing really happened." Amy stared at the entrance to the service area, her gaze wistful. "We just didn't have that spark. Sometimes you just don't feel it, you know?"

Kat's mind veered toward Andrew. In all the chaos of that afternoon she had almost forgotten they had a date scheduled for tonight. The reminder sent a zing of excitement shooting up her spine. They had been together ten months now, and Kat still felt a little giddy every time she thought of him. They definitely weren't lacking that spark in their relationship.

"We're still friends," Amy said. "Or friendly would be more accurate, I guess. There aren't any hard feelings between us, if that's what you want to know."

From Beulah's comments, Kat would have thought the breakup was more contentious. Was Beulah just stirring up trouble, or did DJ harbor some lingering resentment that wasn't present on Amy's side? Perhaps if Kat asked DJ why things had ended he would give her a completely different answer.

Moxie stood up as the front door opened. Andrew and Chief Kenny were entering the showroom, their faces grim. Almost immediately all conversation stopped, and the room plunged into silence.

Kat held her breath as Chief Kenny headed toward the Rockports. "Where's Teddy?" he asked.

Sally Jo blinked. "Teddy?"

"Teddy Poole. Your mechanic." Chief Kenny's jaw tensed. "We need him to answer a few questions."

CHAPTER FIVE

Back at her apartment, Kat absently stroked Tom as she sat in her living room. The brown-and-black cat lay in her lap, purring up a storm. Kat wished she could be so happy, but her brain wouldn't turn off.

"I wonder if Chief Kenny and Andrew arrested Teddy," she said.

Tom looked at her and meowed.

"You think so? They said they only wanted to ask him a few questions. And they didn't make him go down to the station. Wouldn't they have brought him in if they thought he killed Damian?"

Tom tilted his head to the side as though to consider her question.

"And if Teddy did kill Damian, why did he tell everybody about the damaged brake lines?" Kat went on. "Why not just clean up the spilled fluid in Damian's parking spot and hope nobody ever figured out what happened?"

Tom made a noise that sounded like a warble.

Kat ran her hand down his back. "I don't know who did it, Tom. That's the problem."

Matty glanced over at them from where she was sitting on the middle level of the cat tree by the window. The yellow-and-brown tortoise-shell had been camped there for the better part of a week. There had been an unusual amount of bird activity outside that window now that it was breeding season, and Matty seemed loath to miss a single minute of it. A few days ago Kat had even spied a robin chirping at Matty through the glass. The tortoiseshell had gone bonkers. Her eyes had been so large Kat thought they might pop right out of her head, and her teeth had chattered like mad as she released what Kat thought of as the bird meow —those bizarre noises she and Tom always made when they spotted a bird.

A knock on her apartment door snapped Kat back to the present.

"That must be Andrew." She eased Tom off of her lap. "We have a date tonight, but I half figured he'd cancel because of what happened to Damian Rockport. Maybe they got lucky and Teddy confessed."

Tom thwacked his tail against the sofa as if to say he hoped so.

Kat stood up and bounded toward the door, that familiar flutter blooming in her stomach. But when she flung the door open it wasn't Andrew standing in the hallway but Teddy Poole. He no longer wore his work coveralls, but there was no mistaking the man's identity.

Teddy gave her a lopsided smile. "Hello."

Kat mentally smacked herself for not looking through the peephole first. But the Rockport Rides mechanic was the last person she would have expected to pay her a visit.

"If you're wondering why I didn't buzz, I followed someone else into the building," he said, as if that tidbit would help to put her at ease.

Kat was still gaping at him when Tom wandered over. The feline sat down in the doorway and looked up at Teddy, his head cocked to one side.

A smile brightened Teddy's face. "Who's this fella?" He crouched down and made a clucking sound, one hand stretched toward Tom.

Kat's insides tightened. She had half a mind to snatch up Tom and slam the door shut, but before she could act Tom moved out of her reach and closer to Teddy.

She didn't breathe as she watched Tom sniff Teddy's fingers. The grooves in the mechanic's hands were stained with grease, and dirt was caked under his nails, but Tom didn't seem to care. The big cat shoved his nose into Teddy's palm.

Teddy grinned as he pet the cat. "This one's as affectionate as Moxie."

"Tom's a sweetheart," Kat said, finally finding her voice. "But what are you doing here?"

Teddy's smile faded. He stood back up and folded his hands in front of him. "Well, since your friend mentioned your knack for investigating and that you live in Cherry Hills Commons, I decided . . ."

"You decided why not drop by unannounced to see if I could clear your name," Kat filled in.

Teddy nodded.

Thanks a lot, Imogene, Kat thought. She was going to have to have a word with her friend the next time they talked.

"I'm not sure what you expect me to do,"

Kat said out loud. "I'm not a cop. Nor am I a licensed private investigator."

"I don't care what you are as long as you can keep me from getting fired or going to jail for something I didn't do."

"That's asking an awful lot."

"I know. But I don't know where else to turn. Sally Jo already told me not to bother coming back to work until this thing is resolved." Teddy appealed to her with earnest eyes. "I can't afford to lose that job, Ms. Kat. There aren't many mechanic positions available around here, and I have a lot of bills to pay."

Kat felt herself softening. "If I look into this thing I'm going to follow the evidence wherever it takes me. And whatever I find will be turned over to the cops, even if it leads to you."

He bobbed his head. "I wouldn't have it any other way. But whatever you find won't lead to me."

She squinted at him. "You sound awfully confident."

"That's because I'm innocent."

With his self-assured posture and the way he held her gaze she was inclined to believe him. Plus, he did seem genuinely fond of Tom— a definite point in his favor. Kat didn't trust anyone who didn't like animals. And she would hate to see a fellow animal lover end up in prison over something he didn't do because she'd refused to help him.

Oh, who was she kidding? She was too curious to turn the guy away without at least hearing his side of the story. Imogene was right. She was an incorrigible snoop.

Kat gestured for him to enter. "You might as well come in for a minute."

"Thank you."

As Teddy loped past her, Kat caught a whiff of cigarette smoke. She wouldn't be surprised if he had chain-smoked a pack on his way over here. Her boss was a smoker, and Kat knew she tended to light up more under stress. And what could be more stressful than being accused of murder?

Kat closed the door and followed Teddy into the living room, Tom marching between them. "What did the police ask you at the dealership earlier?" she said.

"They wanted to know a bunch of stuff about Mr. Rockport's car. Where he parks, what I look for when I'm doing my weekly service checks, which bay I had it in this morning."

"Did they give you any indication they think

you're the person who cut his brake lines?" Kat asked.

"Yeah." Teddy looked pained as he perched on the edge of one sofa. "They took my fingerprints."

Kat sat on the couch opposite him. "I think that's pretty standard. It doesn't mean they think you did it."

"Maybe, but I just know the Rockports are going to try to blame me. I'm not one of them, and the Rockport gang, they stick together."

Tom hopped onto the couch next to Teddy. But rather than crawl into Teddy's lap as he normally did when he found a warm body to sit on, he jumped onto the back of the sofa where he proceeded to stare at their visitor with unblinking, green eyes. Kat wondered if it was the stench of cigarettes that had prompted Tom to keep his distance.

Or was Tom getting a bad vibe from this man?

Kat shook the thought away. Tom had proven more than once that he was hardly a good judge of criminal character.

She faced Teddy again. "As far as the police go, I would think not being a Rockport is a point in your favor. As an outsider you don't have anything to gain from Damian's death. Sally Jo and DJ, on the other hand, probably both stand to inherit something."

"Huh." Teddy scraped underneath one fingernail using his thumbnail. "I didn't think of that."

"But if one of them did it, it means they had to have mucked around with Damian's car at some point. Did you see either of the Rockports in the service area this morning when you had Damian's car there for its regular tune-up?"

Teddy screwed up his face. "I don't recall seeing them. But I'm not in the shop all the time. They could have gone out there when I was taking a smoke break."

Tom gave the man a sniff as if to assess the veracity of his story. Turning to Kat, he offered her a slow blink. She figured that meant Teddy's smoke break claim held up, at least from Tom's point of view.

"Maybe you could ask Amy if she saw anyone in the shop," Teddy said. "She likes to hang out there sometimes."

"She does?" Kat pictured the young brunette in her head. "What business does Amy have out there?"

"She doesn't." Teddy used his newly cleaned

fingernail to scratch the bridge of Tom's nose. "I'm pretty sure she comes in to watch me work. I think she has the hots for me. She used to go out with DJ, you know, but she broke up with him right after I started working for Mr. Rockport four months ago. I guess she wanted to be free to pursue me, although she waited a respectable amount of time before she started showing up in the shop."

Kat scrutinized him, trying to gauge whether that was male ego talking. But Teddy didn't look smug about being the subject of Amy's supposed crush. And he'd spoken without inflection, as if simply stating facts.

But was Teddy's conclusion the truth? Given what had happened to Damian, perhaps catching Teddy's eye wasn't Amy's true motive for visiting the service area at all. Perhaps she had been waiting for an opportunity to tamper with the boss's car.

"Teddy, did Amy and Damian get along?" Kat asked.

"Yeah, I guess. But not many people didn't get along with Mr. Rockport."

"So you don't think she had any motive to kill him?"

"Amy? Not that I know of."

"What about your other coworkers? Can you think of anyone who might have wanted to harm Damian?"

Teddy scratched Tom's chin. "Nope, not a one."

Kat sat back against the sofa. "Well, somebody had it in for him."

Matty emitted that strangled half meow, half croak from her perch on the cat tree. The tortoiseshell had her neck craned toward the window next to her, her tail beating against one of the tree's sisal posts. With her nose practically pressed to the glass, she fell silent for a moment before her mouth began twitching again, the same broken bird meow emerging from her throat once again.

Teddy's eyes widened in alarm. "What's wrong with her?"

"Nothing," Kat replied. "That's what she does when she spies a bird outside the window."

"Oh. It looks very strange, like she's having some kind of seizure."

"Haven't you ever seen Moxie making bird noises before?"

Teddy shook his head. "I'm usually out in the shop, and Moxie doesn't go out there. Sometimes it can be loud, especially if more than one of us is working."

Kat leaned forward. "More than one person works in the service area?"

"Yeah. Mr. Rockport has a few part-time guys in addition to me. But they weren't there today."

Kat figured that meant they had no opportunity to sabotage Damian's car.

"Are you positive you didn't see anyone else in the service area today?" Kat asked.

"Yeah." Teddy's hand stilled. "But maybe whoever did it never went in the shop. Could be they waited until I drove the car around to Mr. Rockport's parking spot behind the building. He's got this shady area he likes back there, away from everything else."

While Kat could appreciate the value of a shady parking spot in June, Damian's propensity to leave his car in a low-traffic area meant there probably weren't any witnesses if that was where his killer had gained access to his car.

Tom eyed Teddy's limp hand as if he were puzzling out why his massage had ended. He must have decided he hadn't done enough to encourage their visitor, because he started rubbing first his right, then his left cheek against Teddy's fingers. Teddy got the hint and snapped back into action.

Even from here Kat could see the grime em-
bedded deep in the crevices of Teddy's hands.
In his line of work you could probably never get
your hands completely clean.

The fake pink fingernails of Sally Jo
Rockport-Dubois popped into her head. Kat had
a hard time picturing a person with nails like
that being very skilled at manual labor. And she
didn't recall seeing any grease stains on Sally
Jo's yellow sundress, although she supposed
Sally Jo could have thrown a pair of the dealership's coveralls over her clothes or changed
after the fact.

In her sky-high stilettos, Beulah seemed
equally unlikely to mess with a car's brake lines.
And nobody at the dealership had mentioned
seeing her on the premises before the wreck. If
Beulah were guilty she must have sneaked behind the building to where Damian kept his car
parked without anyone spotting her.

Then there was Amy, who struck Kat as the
most likely of the three women to get her hands
dirty. Except, as far as Kat knew, Amy didn't
have much of a motive.

But there was one other person to consider,
someone who had both motive and opportunity

—DJ Rockport. As Damian's son, DJ surely stood to gain something from his father's death, whether it be a stake in the dealership or a monetary inheritance. And it wouldn't have been difficult for him to duck behind the building to where Damian was parked when he wasn't waiting on clients out in the car lot.

The only question left to answer was, did he really do it?

CHAPTER SIX

Andrew stared at Kat with an incredulous expression. "Teddy Poole was here? In your apartment?"

She nodded. "He must have come over after Sally Jo told him he wasn't welcome at the dealership right now."

"I don't like that one bit." Andrew raked his fingers through his sandy blond hair. "What did he want?"

"He wanted me to know he didn't kill Damian Rockport."

"Why is he telling you that?"

"I guess he heard I might have assisted with solving a crime or two before and wanted my help looking into things."

Andrew scowled, a reaction that caused Tom's ears to rotate sideways. The big cat had come running as soon as their visitor had stepped into the apartment. He knew Andrew was always good for a belly rub.

Except, right now Andrew looked too annoyed to pay any attention to Tom. Kat probably should have waited until he was sitting down before announcing that a potential killer had popped in for a chat.

She expelled a breath. "Andrew, I'm fine. Teddy didn't hurt me. He wanted my help."

"He shouldn't have been here at all." Andrew stepped over Tom and strode to the center of the living room. "And you shouldn't have let him in. You have no business getting involved."

Irritation flared inside Kat. "Well, he was right about me helping to solve a few crimes."

"Yes, and you've put yourself in danger more than once. I don't like you being in harm's way."

"That might not be your choice."

Andrew stomped toward the other side of the room. When he reached the wall he spun around and glared at Kat. She jammed her hands on her hips and glared right back at him. She despised when people told her what to do, even if they might be kinda sorta right.

Matty peeked at the humans from her spot on the cat tree. She must have decided they weren't as interesting as the birds because she turned back toward the window a second later.

Andrew started pacing back toward the opposite side of the living room. Tom hurried after him, meowing with an urgency that Kat couldn't decipher. Did he want attention, or was Tom warning Andrew against bossing his human around?

If Tom's meow was a warning, Andrew didn't take heed.

"You need to stay out of it, Kat," he said, stopping so abruptly that Tom collided with his leg.

Tom recovered quickly, rubbing his face against the cuff of Andrew's slacks as if that was what he had intended to do all along. He wound his way between Andrew's ankles, then flopped onto the carpet and stretched out to his full length.

"Right now Poole is our prime suspect," Andrew said, not even glancing at Tom. "All we're waiting for is something concrete to tie him to that leaky brake line before we officially arrest him."

"You mean you're waiting for fingerprint results," Kat said.

Andrew nodded.

"You realize his prints are going to be all over that car," Kat told him. "He was in charge of servicing it. In fact, he looked at it just this morning."

"So he's said."

Tom lifted his head and yowled, clearly unhappy about being ignored.

Taking pity on the poor, neglected feline, Kat stooped down to pet him. "You know, Teddy was the one who first brought up the possibility of Damian being murdered. He said there's no way foul play isn't involved."

"So?"

"So if he were guilty why wouldn't he try to blame the crash on a manufacturing defect?"

"Because he knew we wouldn't buy it," Andrew said. "And when we got the car down to the lab and found out what really happened he would only look more guilty for lying to us."

Kat frowned, her gaze on Tom as if he might help to clarify things. "I don't know."

"Guilty people drawing attention to evidence is not unheard of, Kat. And it doesn't mean Poole is innocent."

"It doesn't mean he's guilty either."

Andrew slumped onto the sofa and crossed his arms over his chest. "Why are you fighting me on this?"

"I don't know. He just strikes me as innocent, that's all. And if you ask me, Damian Rockport's family had a lot more to gain from his death than Teddy."

"Oh, I can't argue with you there." Andrew stared at her for a moment before his face softened. "Look, we're not trying to railroad this guy, if that's what you're thinking."

She nodded, some of the fight leaving her system. "I know. You're a good cop."

"And trust me, if we find one of the other Rockports' prints where they shouldn't be, we'll be turning our focus on them."

"But in the meantime, Teddy's your guy."

Andrew nodded, sending a chunk of his hair falling over his eyes. He shoved it back into place with one hand.

The gesture made Kat's heart ache. It was a classic Andrew move, one she found both alluring and warmly familiar.

She sighed. Why did they have to be spending such a pleasant Saturday evening arguing over a suspicious death? She would much rather have spent their time together enjoying a nice meal or watching a movie—or doing anything, really, that wouldn't pit them against each other on opposite sides of her living room.

Something bit Kat's hand. She hadn't realized until then that she'd stopped petting Tom. She gave his side a scratch, but evidently she wasn't the person he wanted. He jumped up and circled around to the other side of the coffee table, where he could sit by Andrew's feet and stare at him.

Andrew finally acknowledged the cat. He patted his leg, and Tom leaped into his lap. The feline turned around until he had a good view of the living room, then folded himself into a loaf shape. With his eyes already slipping closed, he looked as if he could stay like that for hours.

Andrew didn't look at Kat as he plucked a cat hair from his shirt. "I probably shouldn't be telling you this, but Teddy Poole was observed to have been arguing with Rockport several times in the past couple of weeks."

It took Kat a moment to realize he was offering her case information, something he rarely did. "He was?" she asked.

"Sally Jo says Rockport had issues with Poole's work. I gather Poole is a rather sloppy mechanic."

"Sloppy enough to have damaged a car's brake lines without noticing what he'd done?" she mused aloud.

"It's possible. We've heard secondhand that Rockport had some serious issues with Poole's work recently. Sally Jo claims he'd even been considering letting the guy go."

Kat dropped onto the couch next to Andrew. "No wonder he's your number one suspect."

"If Poole's carelessness is what got Rockport killed he won't be guilty of murder, but he could still be facing some serious charges."

Kat considered another possibility. Could Teddy have intentionally cut those brake lines because he feared Damian Rockport was on the verge of firing him, then come over here with that story about being innocent in the hopes of getting her to pin his crime on someone else?

The thought didn't make Kat happy. And if that was Teddy's intent he would be in for a big surprise. Because, like Andrew, she had no intention of railroading an innocent person.

She just wished she knew who in this case was innocent and who was guilty.

CHAPTER SEVEN

Andrew left Kat's apartment shortly after telling her about Damian Rockport's issues with Teddy's job performance. Kat let him go without protest. Despite how they had originally planned to spend the evening together, she hadn't been in a date mood after their spat, and she suspected Andrew felt the same. Instead, she'd gone to bed early with Teddy and the rest of the Rockport Rides crew still on her mind. Her dreams had been more like nightmares, featuring horrific car accidents and lots of cryptic Southern idioms.

She woke up Sunday morning determined to pay another visit to the auto dealership. She knew she wouldn't be able to rest until she did

everything possible to identify the person responsible for Damian's crash.

She half expected the dealership to be
closed, but when she pulled into the lot that
afternoon the building lights were on. She
parked near the entrance, surprised to see Imogene getting out of the car next to her.

"Hi, Imogene," Kat said, climbing out of her
own vehicle.

"Kat!" Imogene smiled as she closed her car
door. "What are you doing here?"

Kat wasn't sure how to respond. Although
she was here on a sleuthing mission—and, in
small part, in stubborn defiance to Andrew's
orders—she didn't want to admit as much.

Imogene opened her passenger door and
lifted a huge foil-covered dish from the seat. "I
suppose you're here for the same reason I am,
to pay my respects."

"Yes, my respects." Kat figured that was as
good an excuse as any. "But you're much better
prepared than me. I didn't think to bring food."

Imogene chuckled. "Yes, well, I'm also a
much better cook than you."

Kat laughed with her. "I can't argue with
that."

"I made Sally Jo my vegan potato casserole."

"Sounds delicious."

"I had to do something. Poor Sally Jo is devastated." Imogene eyed Kat as they headed toward the building. "Or do you think she killed him?"

Kat almost tripped on a sidewalk crack. "Why would I think that?"

"Oh, Kat." Imogene looked around before leaning closer and lowering her voice. "You can admit it. You're here to snoop around, aren't you?" She winked, a knowing smile on her face.

Kat couldn't help but grin. "You know me too well, Imogene."

"Well, I can't say I blame you. I'll even admit I'm not averse to learning a bit more about Damian's fate myself. From everything Kenny has told me, it seems extremely likely that *accident* was precipitated by somebody who works here."

Since they had reached the entrance to the dealership, Kat didn't reply. She held the door open, letting Imogene enter first. Moxie stood up from where he'd been resting on the hood of one of the showroom cars and jumped to the floor to come greet them.

"Hey, Moxie," Imogene said as the cat approached. "Aren't you the cutest thing ever?"

Moxie lifted his tail up in acknowledgment while he walked the final few steps in their direction. He sat down by Imogene's feet and tilted his face up, his nose twitching.

"I guess I'm not the only one who thinks that casserole smells delicious," Kat said, reaching down to run her hand over Moxie's head.

Amy waved from the beverage station. "Hello, ladies. Welcome back to Rockport Rides."

"Thank you," Imogene replied. She and Kat went over to join Amy. "Honestly, I wasn't sure if you'd be open today after yesterday's horrendous tragedy."

Amy's eyes grew moist, and her head dropped to the paper cup in her hands. "DJ wanted to close for the day, but Mrs. Rockport-Dubois said she needed something to keep her mind occupied."

"I can certainly understand that," Imogene said.

Kat could understand the need to stay busy too, but in this case she couldn't help but wonder if Sally Jo wasn't keeping the dealership open as a distraction from grief so much as because she was thrilled to finally have full control over the business.

Imogene held up the casserole dish. "I brought this for Sally Jo and DJ. Are they here?"

"Mrs. Rockport-Dubois is in the back office. DJ took a potential client out on a test drive."

Imogene smiled. "So I guess you're holding down the fort."

"I guess so." Amy didn't sound very enthused over the idea.

Imogene set her casserole on the counter near the fountain machine. With her back still toward Amy, she shot Kat a look and angled her head sideways. Kat got the message. This would be the perfect time to coax more information out of the Rockport Rides employee.

Kat cleared her throat. "So, uh, Amy. What's going to happen with Rockport Rides now that Damian is dea . . . has passed away?"

"I'm sure there will be some changes, but I'd be surprised if Mrs. Rockport-Dubois doesn't keep the place open. Like I said before, she has a lot of good business ideas."

"Is she inheriting the dealership?" Kat asked.

"Either her or DJ."

"So they'll be equal partners?"

Amy shrugged. "I don't know the breakdown, but I doubt it matters. Those two have always acted as a team."

Kat was vaguely aware that Moxie had hopped onto the counter at some point and was now sniffing at one corner of Imogene's casserole. But she didn't pay any attention to the cat, her thoughts elsewhere. It occurred to her that Sally Jo and DJ might be partners in not only the business but in how they'd gained control of that business as well. The possibility of them being in cahoots made so much sense she wasn't sure why she hadn't considered it before. After all, who better to provide you with an airtight alibi than your partner in crime? And if the police managed to determine when exactly Damian's brake lines had been cut, Kat wouldn't doubt the duo would lie for each other without a second thought.

But that still meant one of them had to have found an opportunity to physically tamper with Damian's sedan.

"Amy," Kat said, "does DJ know a lot about cars?"

Amy's lips curved upward. "Well, sure. He knows everything about every vehicle we have here on the lot."

"So if he needed to, say, give one a tune-up,

he would know how to do that?"

"Oh, I wouldn't go that far. When I said he knows everything I meant he can tell you about the features that come with every car. But he doesn't actually work on them."

"Did you ever see him in the service area the times you were out there?"

Amy's brow furrowed. "What makes you think I would be out there?"

"Teddy told me you hang out there sometimes." Kat paused. "Was he mistaken?"

Amy blushed as her eyes skirted toward the service area door. "I might go back there every now and then—same as everybody else around here—but I would hardly say I hang out there."

The look of longing in Amy's eyes made Kat think she would have loved to have spent more time back there if only Teddy had ever made her feel welcome. Kat wondered why Teddy had never encouraged Amy's feelings. Did he not find her attractive, or did his disinterest stem from the fact that she used to date the boss's son? Should a romance have ever blossomed between them it would have undoubtedly put him in an awkward position.

But Kat wasn't here to troubleshoot why Amy's interest wasn't reciprocated.

"So DJ never went into the service area, as far as you know?" Kat said, getting back to her original question.

"Well, obviously he goes in there. It's not exactly a private place. But I can't see him working on cars." Amy ran one finger around the lip of her cup. "DJ's a born and bred salesman. He's much better at working his mouth than his hands."

Imogene's eyebrows shot up her forehead. Looking at her, Kat had to squelch a snicker. Although Amy's words were certainly suggestive, Kat didn't think the young woman had intended them as innuendo.

A crinkling noise alerted them to a situation on the counter. Moxie was standing next to Imogene's potato casserole with one paw in the air as he took tentative jabs at the foil covering.

"Moxie!" Imogene yanked the dish out of his reach. "That's not for you, silly boy."

Moxie stood on his hind feet and curled his front paws close to his chest.

Amy grinned. "He's a trip, isn't he?"

"He sure is," Imogene said with a laugh.

"He's been particularly feisty today," Amy said. "I don't know if it's because Mr. Rockport isn't here, or because he got to spend the night in a real house."

"Where does Moxie usually sleep?" Kat asked.

"Here at the dealership." Amy shifted her cup between her hands so she could massage the cat's ears. "But now that Mr. Rockport is gone, Mrs. Rockport-Dubois says she plans to take him home every night."

Kat recalled DJ mentioning his father's allergies. With Damian out of the picture it seemed as if Sally Jo was not only the business's primary decision maker but also the new head of household.

Now if only Kat could determine exactly how far Sally Jo had been willing to go to secure her newfound independence.

CHAPTER EIGHT

Amy didn't seem inclined to chat more, pointing Imogene and Kat to Sally Jo's office before turning her back on them as she refilled her cup from the soda machine. Kat got the hint, as did Imogene. They both began walking.

As soon as Moxie saw they were on the move, the feline darted in front of them. He stayed two steps ahead all the way across the sales floor.

The office door was slightly ajar. Moxie pushed his way in, widening the opening enough for Kat to glimpse Sally Jo seated behind the desk inside.

Imogene adjusted the casserole dish in her

hands and rapped on the doorframe. "Knock, knock," she called out.

Sally Jo looked up. "Imogene!"

Beulah stood up from one of the guest chairs. "Why, lookie here, Sally Jo. She's done brought enough food to last you till the Second Comin'. You'll be fat as a tick by the end of the week."

Imogene handed Beulah the casserole dish. "It was the least I could do to show you all how very sorry I am for what happened yesterday."

"Well, that's mighty kind of you." Beulah set the dish on the desk and peeled one corner of the foil back. "Sally Jo, don't that look more scrumptious than a cowboy in his birthday finest?"

Sally Jo barely glanced at the potato cas- serole before her eyes returned to the papers on the desk. "It sure does."

Beulah's ruby-red lips puckered. "Y'all will have to excuse my sister. She's had her nose buried in those books before the rooster even had a chance to crow this mornin'. Keepin' busy always has been the Dubois way of copin' with tragedy."

Imogene smiled. "I completely understand. And since you must have a lot to do, I can see myself out."

"Nonsense. My mama would turn over in her grave if a Dubois woman sent a visitor packin' without showin' them some ol'-fashioned Southern hospitality." Beulah bustled over to them and looped one arm through Imogene's and the other through Kat's. "We'll go chitchat on the sales floor."

Beulah steered them out of the office and toward one of the empty sales desks near the window, leaving a floral-scented trail in her wake. Moxie held his head and tail high as he trotted ahead of them, and Kat wondered if he thought of himself as king of the castle now that Damian was out of the picture.

Amy was still lounging in the beverage area, but as soon as she spotted Beulah she hurried back to her office. She kept her head down, her beverage cup clutched in her hands.

Beulah's eyes trailed the brunette. When Amy's door closed Beulah leaned close to Imogene and whispered loudly enough for Kat to hear, "That girl is trouble with a capital *t*."

"She seemed perfectly pleasant to me," Imogene said.

"Yes, well, pleasant is her job. But as little as she's on the phones that one would have a hard time sellin' a sandbox to a cat with the runs."

Moxie looked at Beulah, his head cocked to one side. Kat didn't know if he were more puzzled or offended by Beulah's choice of words.

Beulah fluffed her hair. "That girl's always millin' 'round where she don't belong. Why, she's worse than a goose flyin' north for the winter. First thing I told Sally Jo to do now that she's in charge 'round here is to cut that one loose. Would serve her right after what she did to Damian Junior."

"I thought DJ was okay with the breakup," Kat said.

Beulah emitted the most ladylike snort Kat had ever heard. "As okay as Cooter Brown would be partin' ways with Jim Beam! Now, Damian Junior might not be one to pitch a hissy fit, but he was right near heartbroken when that gal dumped him quicker'n a sack of garbage on trash day."

Moxie had taken to twining between Kat's ankles. She assumed he wanted attention, but he shied away when she bent down to pet him. He waited until she straightened back up before resuming his figure eights around her feet.

"Like I said yesterday," Beulah went on, "Damian—may he rest in peace—should've tossed that one out the door when he had the chance. But don't y'all worry your pretty little heads over it. Sally Jo's fixin' to whip things into shape 'round here. That one'll be the first to go —that one and that other one in the back, too."

"You mean Teddy?" Kat asked.

"Mmm-hmm." Beulah peered around as if to make sure they were still alone before hunching closer. "Sally Jo and I just had ourselves a nice little chat 'bout him. Did y'all know she told him to stay home until further notice? Between us gals, Sally Jo believes that one's elevator has stalled out on the second floor, bless his heart."

"I'm not sure what that means," Kat admitted.

"Then let me rephrase it for you, honey. Lately Teddy's been makin' more mistakes than a surgeon with a chainsaw. Sally Jo says he hasn't always been this bad, but he's gettin' to be as good at fixin' cars as a dog is at jugglin' tin cans. I gather Damian even had to exchange a few words with him on the subject these past coupla weeks." Beulah's lips thinned. "It certainly makes one wonder whether he might've had a hand in what happened to poor old Damian, may he rest in peace."

Imogene laid her hand on Beulah's arm.

"I'm sure the police are investigating that angle."

"I sure do hope so. Meanwhile, Sally Jo's fixin' to secure a replacement for him quick as can be. She can't be frettin' over whether somethin' like this might happen again, even if Teddy swears like a sailor docked at the wrong port that he ain't got nothin' to do with Damian's wreck."

Moxie had abandoned Kat and now stood with his back arched against Imogene's leg. When Imogene stretched her hand toward him he darted out of reach, then dashed right back to her. This time he let her pet him.

"Beulah," Kat said, tearing her eyes away from the frisky feline, "you said Teddy's performance problems only cropped up recently?"

"Not me, that's what Sally Jo says," Beulah replied.

"Does Sally Jo have any idea why Teddy has been so careless lately?"

"We didn't get into all that. But I'll bet my last nickel it has somethin' to do with a card-carryin' member of our fair sex. Didn't y'all see how he was checkin' out the twins yesterday?" Beulah patted her cleavage. "And when a man starts lettin' his south side run things, you can be darn sure it won't be long 'fore his work starts stinkin' as bad as a polecat with a burr up its bum."

Could Amy's visits to the service area be to blame for Teddy's recent mistakes? Kat wondered. Teddy had said she'd only started venturing back there fairly recently. Maybe he found her presence so distracting he had difficulty focusing on work when she was around.

Although, Kat probably shouldn't take the Rockports' disparaging talk about Teddy's work at face value. It could be their way of deflecting suspicion from themselves. If they could paint Teddy as a careless employee, it would be that much easier to implicate him in Damian's death.

That brought up another question to consider. Would Sally Jo and DJ have confided in Beulah if they had conspired to commit murder? Probably, Kat decided. At least, she was fairly certain Sally Jo would have said something. She and Beulah were obviously a tight-knit duo.

"You know," Kat said, eyeing Beulah carefully, "I never had a sister. Sally Jo's lucky that way. She must be relieved to have you around in her time of crisis."

Beulah straightened her spine. "Our mama raised us to be each other's legs when one of us goes lame. And with Damian gone Sally Jo's bound to need a little more help 'round here."

"Are you going to be joining the business?" Imogene asked.

"I sure am, sugar. Sally Jo's got more ideas than a man in a bordello, but she's gonna need a right-hand lady to help execute them. I can give her a right good dose of confidence at the same time—her and Damian Junior. As well as he provided for her, that's one thing Sally Jo ain't never got from Damian, may he rest in peace."

"Damian always did have his own mind," Imogene concurred.

"Whoo-wee, honey. You're tellin' me!" Beulah clucked her tongue. "Stubborn as a mule, that one. Sally Jo kept tellin' him he needed to teach Damian Junior how to run the business so he wouldn't be flounderin' when it came time for him to take over, but Damian never did pay her no mind. Bring up any topic under the sun, and that man always had more to say than a sinner in Sunday confessional. But ask him to show you his books and he'd clam right up. And now look what's happened. Sally Jo and Damian Junior have been left high and dry with nary a clue what to do 'round here. But they'll be all right. My sister's got a right good head on her shoulders, and Damian Junior's the same way. Smart as a whip, that nephew of mine."

As if she had conjured him from thin air, DJ stepped into the dealership. Moxie rocketed toward him with a speed that made it clear he hadn't forgotten about DJ spilling that bag of treats yesterday.

"Well, I do declare, there's Damian Junior now." Beulah waved her arms as vigorously as any drowning woman would. "Damian Junior, you c'mon over here and give your Auntie Beulah a great big ol' hug!"

DJ hesitated, his eyes darting back toward the door as if he were debating making a run for it.

"What're you waitin' for, boy?" Beulah set her hands on her hips. "Time's a tickin'."

Kat thought she saw DJ sigh before he started in their direction.

"Hi, Aunt Beulah," he said without any enthusiasm. "What brings you here today?"

"Why, you and your mama, of course. Had to make sure y'all're okay."

Before DJ could reply, Beulah grabbed him by the shoulders and pulled him into a tight embrace. When he finally managed to squirm free, Beulah eyed him with an assessing look.

"How're you holdin' up, Damian Junior?" she asked.

"All right," he said.

Beulah flapped her hand at Imogene and Kat. "I was just tellin' these fine ladies here 'bout how you got more horse sense than a two-headed mare."

DJ toed the tile floor. "I wish you wouldn't brag on me so much, Aunt Beulah. I'm not any smarter than anyone else."

"Hogwash! You're the brightest boy I know. And once you and your mama start lettin' yourselves shine y'all're gonna be Uncle Sam's best buddies come tax time. People are gonna come flockin' in here like ducks to a June bug convention. Y'all just wait and see. Business is gonna be ten times what it ever was when your daddy was runnin' the place, may he rest in peace."

DJ blushed, clearly embarrassed by his aunt's lavish praise.

Or, Kat thought with a little shiver, was that guilt that had turned his face red and kept him from meeting any of their gazes?

CHAPTER NINE

Beulah excused herself shortly after DJ showed up, claiming she had more to do today than 'a moth in a mitten factory.' Having developed a low-grade headache after listening to the woman for the past twenty minutes, Kat hadn't even tried to decipher this latest expression.

"So," DJ said as soon as Beulah left the showroom, "whaddaya say I show you two ladies some more cars?"

"I wish I could stay, but I've got an appointment to get to," Imogene said, hurrying toward the door. "I'll come back later this week when I have more time."

Imogene didn't even stop to give Moxie

a goodbye pat before slipping outside. Kat couldn't blame her for her hasty departure. That predatory glint was back in DJ's eye.

"Looks like it's just you and me," DJ said, grinning at Kat. "Whaddaya say we head on out to the lot and see if we can't put you in a new ride before the day is over?"

The last thing Kat wanted was to have to ward off an unwanted sales pitch. But given that she and DJ were the only people left in the showroom, she forced herself to stay put. She might not get another chance to question him alone.

DJ walked over to the window and tapped on the glass. "That's your car there, isn't it?"

"Yes." Since there were no other cars in the customer parking area, Kat figured there was no point in denying it.

"Looks like it could fall apart any day now. But we could give you a good trade-in price."

Kat tapped her chin as if she were seriously considering his offer. "Hmm."

"I bet we could find you a great new set of wheels that will barely put a dent in your wallet." DJ rubbed his fingertips together as though he could already feel Kat's money in his hands. "We have some real steals available right now."

"I did see a couple cars that appealed to me yesterday."

DJ practically salivated. "Yeah?"

"But before I look at them I'd like some assurance that your maintenance personnel know what they're doing here."

The smile slid off of DJ's face. He stared out the window, the eager glint in his eye replaced by a dull, lifeless patina.

Moxie must have sensed DJ's shift in mood. The black cat rubbed his cheeks and sides against DJ's legs as though to offer him comfort.

Kat forged on despite the pinch of guilt she felt over dredging up his father's accident. "After what happened to Mr. Rockport, I'm concerned about how well you look after your cars here. Can you guarantee what happened yesterday won't happen again?"

DJ's jaw was tight when he turned to face her. "That was a targeted attack."

"Are you sure about that? Your aunt seems to think Mr. Rockport's accident was the result of Teddy Poole's negligence."

"Aunt Beulah got that idea from Mama. But Teddy didn't cause that accident. He wouldn't have been that careless."

"So what do you think happened?"

DJ shrugged before his shoulders sagged. "I don't have a clue. But somebody clearly had it out for my dad."

Sitting at home thinking about Damian's death, DJ had been near the top of Kat's suspect list. But looking at the dejection in his face now, the doubts were creeping in.

But she couldn't forget DJ's effortless ability to switch from dogged car salesman to meek Southern boy. She'd witnessed the transition herself both yesterday and today, and it forced her to question whether DJ might have a few other personalities he kept hidden. Perhaps he even had a dangerous, lethal side perfectly capable of plotting the death of a close family member.

Sally Jo came out of her office. She started toward the beverage station but changed course when she saw Kat and DJ standing on the other side of the room.

"Well, hey there," she said to Kat, a warm smile on her face. "Welcome back to Rockport Rides."

"Thank you," Kat said, although she was a bit puzzled by the greeting. Had Sally Jo already forgotten about Kat's appearance in her office? Or maybe the new widow hadn't noticed her earlier. She had seemed rather preoccupied.

Moxie jogged over to Sally Jo and listed against her leg.

Sally Jo blew an air kiss in Moxie's direction before addressing DJ. "Son, you treat this one here right," she said, nodding at Kat. "When she finds herself a car she fancies, you give her the best deal to be found on this side of the Mason-Dixon line."

DJ touched Sally Jo's elbow. "I will, Mama."

Kat shifted, hoping he wouldn't start in on his sales spiel again. With two Rockports tag-teaming her, it would be that much more difficult to steer the conversation back to Damian.

Sally Jo cocked her head to one side. "DJ, you been out in the shop recently?"

He shook his head. "I was outside with a customer until two minutes ago. Why?"

"'Cause it sounds deader than a church on Mardi Gras back there."

DJ crossed his arms over his chest. "Well, what did you expect when you told Teddy not to come in today? You know you're punishing him for something he didn't do, right?"

The offhand way that Sally Jo dismissed his

comment with a wave of her pink fingernails gave Kat the impression this wasn't the first time they were disagreeing about Teddy's forced absence. Maybe the two weren't as tight of a team as Amy had claimed.

Their dispute also compelled Kat to reconsider the possibility of a criminal partnership between the two. If they had conspired to murder Damian, wouldn't they both be on the same page about setting up Teddy to take the fall?

Sally Jo's lips puckered as she looked at the clock on the wall. "One of the part-timers told me he'd be over quick as he could. Didn't realize it'd take him a month of Sundays. And now Dotty Graham is on her way over here expectin' to get her oil changed before Bible study."

"You could ask Amy to do it," DJ said. "Or are you going to suspend her next?"

Sally Jo gave him a stern look. "Why you're always stickin' up for that girl after what she did to you I'll never understand."

"She didn't do anything to me. It just didn't work out."

"Amy knows how to do oil changes?" Kat interjected.

"That's what she says," Sally Jo replied. "But

after the way she dumped my baby, I don't trust that girl any more than I'd trust a blind man with a huntin' rifle."

DJ exhaled. "Why would she lie about that, Mama?"

"I'm just sayin'." Sally Jo studied DJ for a moment before licking her thumb and rubbing it against his cheek.

DJ recoiled. "Mama!"

"Hold still. You got somethin' on your face."

A black blob zipped past Kat's feet. Moxie was zooming toward one side of the sales floor, his tail twitching like mad. When he reached the floor-to-ceiling window he stopped, his eyes locked on to a pigeon strutting across two empty parking spaces. Pretty soon Moxie's mouth was quivering, the typical feline 'I spy a bird' sound emerging from his throat.

Sally Jo chuckled as she sashayed over to the cat so she could scratch his head with her long fingernails. "Oh, Moxie. Look at you. Always wantin' somethin' you can't have."

Moxie didn't appear to hear her, his eyes still trained out the window.

But Kat heard her. And Sally Jo's words triggered a reassessment of everything she'd learned in the past twenty-four hours.

"Of course," she mumbled, realization slamming into her like a gale-force wind.

"Of course what, honey?" Sally Jo said.

Kat jerked. She hadn't realized she'd spoken loudly enough for anyone to hear. But she supposed it was just as well.

"I just figured out why Damian was killed," Kat said. "And it's because he refused to give someone something they wanted but could never have."

CHAPTER TEN

"Honey, that makes about as much sense as a Catholic preacher readin' the Torah," Sally Jo said, squinting at Kat. "You're sayin' Damian was killed because he had somethin' someone else wanted?"

Kat shook her head. "I'm saying he was killed because he denied somebody something they wanted. Specifically Amy."

"Amy!" The word emerged from Sally Jo's mouth as a high-pitched shout.

DJ stared, slack-jawed, at Kat. His expression didn't look all that different from his mother's, and in that moment Kat could clearly see the resemblance between the two.

Amy poked her head out of her office. "Did

you call for me, Mrs. Rockport-Dubois?"

Sally Jo jumped three feet in the air. "Goodness gracious, great balls of fire! Amy! You nearly made my bladder scatter."

Amy frowned. "Sorry. I thought you yelled my name."

"Well, yes." Sally Jo took a deep breath before leaving Moxie to his bird-watching and starting back toward DJ and Kat. She beckoned to Amy with one hand. "C'mon over here."

Amy headed toward them, her steps halting. She clearly knew something was up.

When she came within a few feet of the group, she stopped. "What can I do for you?" she asked Sally Jo.

Sally Jo jerked her chin toward Kat. "You can listen to what Kat here has to say."

Kat felt a little lightheaded as she turned to face Amy. "Were you the one who severed Damian Rockport's brake lines?"

Amy stiffened. "Wha—Why—I—" She broke off with a squeak.

Moxie must have mistaken Amy's stammering for the human version of the bird meow. The black cat abandoned his post by the window and approached Amy, his head swinging from left to right as he searched for the feathered creature that had left her tongue-tied.

"Teddy told me you were always venturing out into the service area," Kat said. "He thought it was because you had a crush on him, and I assumed the same. It wasn't until DJ said something just now that I realized that's not the case at all."

Amy looked at DJ. "What did you say?"

DJ scratched his head as if trying to remember.

"He said you know how to perform oil changes," Kat answered.

DJ snapped his fingers. "That's right."

"I should have realized earlier," Kat said, playing through both of her previous encounters with Amy. "When we were talking before, I saw you look longingly at the door to the service area. I wrongly thought you were pining over Teddy, but you were really pining over something else. You wish you had his job, don't you? Except Damian would never have put a female mechanic on his payroll."

Nobody breathed as they all waited for Amy to respond. Even Moxie seemed riveted by the suspense. He no longer appeared to be looking for birds, at any rate.

"Mr. Rockport thought women had no

business tinkering with cars," Amy finally said, looking at Moxie as if it were easier to explain herself to him than the humans. "Like I told you yesterday, he was sexist."

"Is that why you killed him?" Kat asked.

Amy shook her head as tears flooded her eyes. "I didn't mean to kill him."

Sally Jo sucked in a noisy breath. DJ wrapped a steadying hand around her waist, and Sally Jo clutched at his shirt as if he might be the only thing keeping her upright.

Amy brushed the tears from her cheeks, but they kept coming. "I didn't mean to kill him," she said again, her voice quavering with emotion. "All I wanted was to be given a shot."

Kat slanted her head. "And how would tampering with Damian's brake lines give you a shot?"

"I thought everyone would think Teddy was responsible. That's why I've been going out into the service area sometimes. I've been looking for opportunities to mess with some of the cars when Teddy wasn't paying attention. I haven't been doing anything serious, just little things here and there like loosening some spark plugs or unscrewing the occasional oil cap. I figured since Teddy is in charge of all that stuff everybody would think he was to blame."

Sally Jo's arms flopped to her sides. "Well slap me silly. *You* did all that?"

Amy nodded.

Moxie's whiskers twitched, a disapproving look on his face. Or maybe that was Kat projecting her own feelings onto the feline.

"But nothing I did was severe enough for Teddy to get more than a warning to be more careful," Amy continued. "So I decided I needed to do something bigger if I wanted to really get Mr. Rockport's attention, something he couldn't ignore. I thought if he had a little scare with his own car he would finally do what he should have done four months ago and given me that mechanic's job instead of hiring Teddy off the street. I didn't think Mr. Rockport would d—d—die!" She choked on the last word before burying her face in her hands.

Moxie sidled closer to her. When Amy pulled her hands away from her face and saw the cat sitting there, she reached down and scooped him up. Moxie put his front paws on her shoulders and licked the tears from her face. Apparently he was too kind of a soul to withhold comfort from a woman in distress, even if he did disapprove of her behavior.

With Moxie in her arms, Amy regained some of her composure. "I never intended for Mr. Rockport to get hurt," she said. "I thought he would get in the car and maybe drive it a couple yards through the parking lot before he realized the brakes weren't working. But I guess I didn't cut through the pipes right and it took longer than it should have for his brake fluid to drain out." She exhaled. "I wish I'd had more time so I could have checked my work. But I knew Teddy would be coming back from his cigarette break at any moment, and I had to work fast before he caught me."

Sally Jo's nostrils flared. "Why, you're more sickenin' than spoiled sweet tea, you know that? Damian gave you a place in his company. He paid you a pretty penny. And how do you show your thanks? You start messin' with his cars and his reputation. And all because he wouldn't give you a dirty, greasy job. If that don't beat all!"

DJ tightened his grip around his mother's waist. Kat wasn't sure if he was hugging or re-straining her. Sally Jo's face had gotten redder and redder with every word out of her mouth, and she looked ready to snap. Kat wouldn't be surprised if she were thinking of using those fake fingernails of hers on Amy's face.

Kat inserted herself between the two women, hoping to put some more distance between them. "What makes you think Damian would have hired you even if he had fired Teddy?" she asked Amy.

"Because I'm ten times the mechanic he is. And I know Mr. Rockport passed me over for that position once, but I thought if he saw that his first choice didn't work out he might soften his stance on only hiring male mechanics. I figured if anybody could get him to change his mindset it would be me, because of my history with the family."

DJ went rigid. "Are you talking about us?"

Amy blushed as she bobbed her head.

"Is that why you agreed to go out with me?" DJ said. "Because you thought Dad would be more inclined to hire you for the position you wanted if we were dating?"

"The thought did enter my mind," Amy admitted. "But that's not why I went out with you. I thought the job might be . . . a bonus."

DJ clenched his teeth. Kat wouldn't blame him for not believing her. It was clear Amy had been willing to go to extremes to get what she wanted.

Amy laid her cheek on Moxie's head. "I

didn't expect any special privileges from your father because I'm a girl or because I dated you, DJ. I really tried to prove my worth to him. Every time we'd talk I'd slip in a little tidbit about engines or transmissions or something, hoping he would realize I was just as knowledgeable about cars as any man. I thought when he saw how much I knew he'd eventually come around and give me a chance."

But of course Damian had never given her the chance she had so desperately wanted. And he had lost his life because of it.

Wracking sobs interrupted Amy's narrative. Sally Jo was no longer in fighting mode. She now had her face pressed against DJ's chest and was bawling as if she were losing Damian all over again.

Kat's heart went out to the woman. How could she have ever suspected this grief-stricken widow of plotting to kill her own husband?

Kat turned away, swallowing the lump developing in her own throat. Pulling out her cell phone, she dialed Andrew's number and waited for him to pick up.

CHAPTER ELEVEN

"Finally, we get to enjoy a nice, quiet night without a case hanging over our heads," Andrew said, smiling at Kat.

Kat smiled back at him, the sight of his dimples warming her heart. She couldn't think of a more perfect start to an evening than the two of them sitting in her living room together. The only thing that would make the situation more perfect was if they were sitting on the same couch. But with Tom nestled on Andrew's lap and Matty curled up on hers, they were trapped unless they were prepared to endure some sad feline looks and guilt-inducing stares.

"What did you want to do tonight?" Kat asked.

"I could take you out to dinner."

"Sounds good. I'm starving."

Andrew scratched Tom's head. "We just need to get these two to free us, and we can be on our way."

Tom made it clear what he thought of that plan. The big cat unfolded himself so he could stretch his body across the full length of Andrew's lap, effectively pinning him to the couch.

Kat had to laugh. "Looks like he's going to make sure you give him a double dose of attention today to make up for how you ignored him last Saturday."

Andrew crooked his head to the side as he bent forward to meet Tom's eye. "Is that true, Tommy?"

Tom meowed before reaching one paw toward Andrew's face. When Andrew didn't back away, the cat lazily hooked two claws inside his left nostril.

"Ack." Andrew worked at freeing himself, but his attempts only made the feline extend his claws farther.

Kat smirked. "And to think all this could have been prevented if only you'd given him one little belly rub the last time you were here."

"Okay, Tom, you've made your point." With

some delicate maneuvering, Andrew finally managed to escape from Tom's hold. He leaned back against the sofa with a sigh of relief. "Remind me not to get too close next time you're mad, buddy."

Tom purred as he rearranged himself. Judging from the way his eyelids were drifting shut, the cat was settling in for a long nap.

Andrew gave Kat a rueful smile. "Speaking of mad, I apologize for trying to tell you what to do last weekend."

"Well, you weren't very successful," Kat replied.

"I was worried about you."

The affection reflected in his blue eyes made Kat's heart swell. "I know. And I appreciate your concern."

They lapsed into a companionable silence, both of them petting their respective felines. Matty started kneading Kat's leg, and Kat thought about when Moxie had comforted Sally Jo in the same manner. Although she was sad for the widow over her loss, she was happy she had Moxie to help soften the blow of losing her husband. Kat hoped they were both adjusting well to Moxie spending nights and evenings inside a real house. Knowing how Tom liked to take over her own bed, she figured they were probably doing all right.

Moxie spending his downtime at Sally Jo's house wasn't the only change in the Rockports' lives. Sally Jo and DJ had been working overtime as they adjusted to the new reality of running Rockport Rides on their own. But Kat had every confidence the two would figure things out—with Beulah's help, of course.

At least the Rockports wouldn't have to get used to a new mechanic. Teddy had been allowed to return to work the day after Amy's confession. Kat was pleased the truth had come out about who was really responsible for all the car problems that had almost gotten an innocent man fired.

As for Amy, it was still unclear how much time she could expect to serve. Although what she had done didn't technically qualify as murder, her actions had still resulted in a man's death. One thing was for sure though. Amy would be facing some serious charges.

Kat's cell phone rang. She steadied Matty with one hand as she stretched toward the coffee table to grab it.

She checked the caller ID before she answered. "Hi, Imogene."

"Kat! Guess what I'm doing."

"I have no idea."

"I'm driving!"

"I hope you're being safe."

Imogene chuckled. "Of course I am. This is hands-free technology. I don't even need to look at the phone to dial. I just tell the car who I want to call, and it does everything for me. It's surreal!"

"That does sound pretty cool." Kat had to smile at the marvel in Imogene's voice. "I take it you're enjoying the new SUV then."

"I'm loving it. I should have traded in my other car ages ago."

"I'm glad it—"

"Kat, I must be off. I've still got half my contact list to get through before I reach my destination."

Kat laughed as Imogene disconnected.

"How's Imogene?" Andrew asked when Kat pulled the phone away from her ear.

"Great." She tossed the phone aside and began petting Matty again. "It sounds like she's enjoying all the features on her new car."

"I'm glad she found something she's happy with."

Kat was glad too. And while Imogene and

Kat's return to the dealership a few days after Amy's arrest had been rather bittersweet, learning what had really happened that fateful Saturday morning hadn't dampened DJ's hungry enthusiasm for selling cars. Watching him in action had been enough to convince Kat that he would eventually recover just fine from the death of his father.

She wondered if there was a Southern expression that encompassed resiliency after a devastating loss. Probably. Sally Jo and Beulah seemed to have a saying for every other occasion. But Kat didn't know how the phrase would go—assuming she'd even understand it if she heard it. So for now she would stick with the less colorful but equally poignant Yankee version.

Life goes on.

NOTE FROM THE AUTHOR

Thank you for visiting Cherry Hills, home of Kat, Matty, and Tom! If you enjoyed their story, please consider leaving a book review on your favorite retailer and/or review site.

Keep reading for an excerpt from Book 24 of the Cozy Cat Caper Mystery series, *Independence Day in Cherry Hills*. Thank you!

INDEPENDENCE DAY *in* CHERRY HILLS

Fourth of July weekend turns deadly in Cherry Hills, Washington when Kat Harper and her police detective boyfriend hear a gunshot in the midst of the neighborhood fireworks. A killer with a grudge has taken advantage of the small-town festivities to shoot a local divorce lawyer in cold blood.

But who committed the murder: a disgruntled divorcé, the lawyer's own unloving wife, or someone else with homicidal tendencies? Kat doesn't know, but the amateur sleuth won't stop investigating until she figures out "whodunit" and the guilty party is celebrating their next holiday behind bars.

* * *

Please check your favorite online retailer for availability.

Excerpt From

INDEPENDENCE DAY *in* CHERRY HILLS

COZY CAT

A

CAPER

MYSTERY
BOOK

24

PAIGE SLEUTH

*B*oom!

    The explosion rang in Katherine Harper's ears and sent her two cats running for safety. Matty and Tom almost collided with each other in their frantic race out of the living room, a scene that might have been comical under different circumstances. But right now Kat was at her wits' end. She would run too if she thought there was any way to escape.

Boom!

And there it was again.

Kat shook her fist at the window from her seat on the sofa. "Enough already!"

Andrew Milhone draped his arm around her shoulders, a wide grin splitting his face and bringing out his adorable twin dimples. "Some-one's in a festive mood."

"I'll be festive on Monday, when it's actually the Fourth of July. But that's still three days away. I don't know if I can take this all week-end."

"It is kind of annoying," Andrew agreed. "But after this it'll be quiet for another six months until New Year's."

"New Year's isn't nearly this bad." Granted, her opinion was based solely upon the most recent New Year's. Although she had grown up in Cherry Hills, she couldn't remember what the local celebrations had been like seventeen years ago when she'd last spent a summer here. The next year had brought with it her high school graduation, legal freedom from the foster care system, and her solemn vow never to return to the small, Central Washington town.

Except she had returned. She still remem-bered that day last July when she'd first run into Andrew after not seeing him for fifteen years. Their reunion had taken place under less than fortunate circumstances, but discovering that her old friend and fellow foster care survivor still lived in town had been a welcome surprise. What had been an even more welcome surprise were the romantic sparks that soon developed between them. By August they were dating, and thanks to Andrew the past eleven months had been some of the happiest ones in her life.

Or maybe she had Matty and Tom to thank for her recent happiness. The two cats had entered her life around the same time as Andrew. How two tiny creatures could bring her so much joy still astonished her. Her heart felt close to bursting every time she thought of them.

But right now the only thing on the verge of bursting was Kat's temper.

Another bang rang out, this one loud enough to rattle her teeth. She nudged Andrew with her elbow. "You're a cop. Can't you flash that badge of yours around and get them to stop?"

"Sorry. Cherry Hills doesn't have any ordinances against setting off fireworks on private property."

"It's still a noise violation, isn't it?"

He drummed his fingers against his thigh. "Tell you what. We'll give them five more minutes. If this continues any longer than that I'll go talk to them, neighbor to neighbor."

Kat bobbed her head. "And if they don't listen, you can shake your handcuffs and threaten to take them down to the station."

Andrew chuckled. "You sure are worked up tonight."

"You saw Matty and Tom. They're scared to death. And there's no telling how many other terrified animals are suffering out there all because a few inconsiderate people want to have fun with pyrotechnics."

Kat pictured Matty and Tom cowering in the shadows of her bedroom. She wished she could explain to them what was going on. The poor things probably thought Cherry Hills was under siege from enemy forces.

She jumped off the couch. "I should go check on the cats."

Before Andrew could reply, she raced down the short hallway to her bedroom. She flicked on the light and looked around, spying Matty's gray-striped tail poking out from underneath the bed. It twitched in short, decisive bursts of motion, a sure sign the tortoiseshell was agitated.

Kat lowered herself to the floor. Lying down, she had a clear view of the yellow-and-brown feline huddled near one of the bed frame's support posts, her green eyes the size of coconuts. Kat reached out to stroke her head.

"It'll be all right, baby. By this time next week all will be quiet again." At least, she certainly hoped that was the case. If this went on for a full week she would have to seriously consider moving.

A soft meow drew Kat's attention to her left. She hadn't noticed him at first, but Tom had also taken refuge under the bed. He was nearly invisible behind the colony of lost cat toys that had slowly been accumulating in the corner for the past eleven months.

"Hey, Tommy." Kat stretched her hand toward him. "Come on over here."

Tom stared impassively back at her. The brown-and-black cat usually relished any opportunity for physical contact, but right now he didn't look inclined to move even for the promise of a belly rub.

"I don't blame you for not budging." Since Matty was the only animal within reach, Kat started petting her again. "If it were up to me, I'd ban fireworks here."

Matty twisted her head around and bit Kat's fingers. Evidently she didn't think their human was doing enough to preserve the peace in their hometown.

"All right, I get the message." Kat withdrew her hand with a sigh. "I'll leave you two alone for now."

She stood up, knowing there was nothing she could do to put them at ease. Still, her heart was heavy as she trudged back to the living room to rejoin Andrew.

"Everything okay?" he asked.

"As well as it can be. They're both hiding under the bed." Kat stood near the edge of the living room, considering. "Think I should slip some food and water under there for them? They might get hungry before things quiet down."

Andrew smirked. "I think you spoil those two enough. But you can do whatever you want."

"I just feel so bad for them. They must think we're in a war zone. Whoever came up with the idea of—"

Another blast sounded, cutting off Kat's words.

Exasperation bubbled up her chest, and the last of her patience snapped. "That's it!" Her hands balled into fists. "If you don't go talk to those people now, I'm going to hunt them down myself. And I probably won't be nearly as nice as you would be."

Andrew didn't appear to hear her. His body had gone rigid, and his jaw was clenched so tightly Kat could see the cords of his facial muscles bunching underneath his skin. Registering the change in his demeanor, her irritation morphed into concern.

"What is it?" she asked.

He raked his fingers through his hair as he stood up and walked over to the window. "Did you hear that?"

"Yeah. I've been listening to this ever since the sun went down at nine. What do you think I've been complaining about for the past hour? It's times like this I wish I knew the mayor or someone in politics. I can't be the only person in Cherry Hills who wants to outlaw fireworks."

"That was no firework." Andrew spun on his heel and strode toward the door. "That was a gunshot."

* * *

Please check your favorite online retailer for availability.

ABOUT THE AUTHOR

Paige Sleuth is a pseudonym for mystery author Marla Bradeen. She plots murder during the day and fights for mattress space with her two rescue cats at night. When not attending to her cats' demands, she writes. Find her at: http://www.marlabradeen.com

Made in United States
Troutdale, OR
08/14/2023

12070573R00083